FEAST FOR 10

CATHRYN FALWELL
CLARION BOOKS, NEW YORK

Clarion Books
a Houghton Mifflin Harcourt Publishing Company imprint
3 Park Avenue, 19th Floor, New York, New York 10016
Text and illustrations copyright © 1993 by Cathryn Falwell
All rights reserved.

For information about permission to reproduce selections from
this book, write to trade.permissions@hmhco.com or to
Permissions, Houghton Mifflin Harcourt Publishing Company,
3 Park Avenue, 19th Floor, New York, New York 10016.
Printed in China

Library of Congress Cataloging-in-Publication Data

Falwell, Cathryn
Feast for 10 / by Cathryn Falwell.
p.   cm.
Summary: Numbers from one to ten are used to tell how
members of a family shop and work together to prepare a meal.
ISBN 0-395-62037-6   PA ISBN 0-395-72081-8
[1. Counting.   2. Afro-Americans—Fiction.   3. Cookery—Fiction.
4. Family life—Fiction.]   I. Title. II. Title: Feast for ten.
PZ7.F198Fe 1993
[E]—dc20
92-35512   CIP   AC

SCP   60   59   58   57   56   55   54   53   52
4500816090

For
my family

in
loving memory
of
my grandmothers

Willie Mae McMullen Chauvin
and
Evelyn Haning Falwell

who often made
feasts for plenty

 **one
cart
into the
grocery
store**

 two
pumpkins
for pie

3 three
chickens
to fry

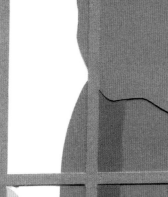

four
children
off to
look for
more

5 five
kinds
of beans

6 six
bunches
of greens

 seven
dill pickles
stuffed in
a jar

8 eight
ripe
tomatoes

9 nine
plump
potatoes

10 ten
hands
help
to load
the car

Then . . .

1 one
car
home
from the
grocery
store

 **two**
will
look

3 three
will
cook

 four
will
taste
and ask
for
more

5 five
empty
cans

6 six
pots and
pans

7 seven
more carrots
to wash
and
peel

8 eight
platters
down

 nine
chairs
around

10 ten
hungry folks
to share
the
meal!